P9-DVO-466

BANJO and RUBY RED

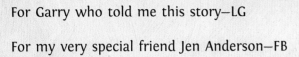

For Garry who told me this story—LG

For my very special friend Jen Anderson—FB

Little Hare Books
an imprint of
Hardie Grant Egmont
Ground Floor, Building 1, 658 Church Street
Richmond, Victoria 3121, Australia

www.littleharebooks.com

Text copyright © Libby Gleeson 2013
Illustrations copyright © Freya Blackwood 2013

First published 2013
Reprinted 2014 (twice)

All rights reserved. No part of this publication
may be reproduced, stored in a retrieval
system or transmitted in any form or by any
means, electronic, mechanical, photocopying,
recording or otherwise, without the prior
written permission of the publisher.

Cataloguing-in-Publication details are available
from the National Library of Australia

978-1-921541-08-7 (hbk.)

Designed by Vida & Luke Kelly
Produced by Pica Digital, Singapore
Printed through Asia Pacific Offset
Printed in Shen Zhen, Guangdong Province, China

7 6 5 4 3

_The illustrations in this book were created using
a combination of laser print on watercolour
paper with oil paints and charcoal._

BANJO and RUBY RED

BY LIBBY GLEESON • ILLUSTRATED BY FREYA BLACKWOOD

LITTLE HARE
www.littleharebooks.com

Old Banjo is the best chook dog we've ever had.

Mum whistles and yells, 'Go, Banjo, go!'

Bark. Bark. Bark.

Squark. Squark. Squark.

Chooks fly up from the grass, down from the trees and out from the shed.

Except Ruby Red.
She sits on top of the woodheap and stares.

Bark. Bark. Bark.
Squark. Squark. Squark.

Chooks fly into their yard, peck at
the ground and settle on their roosts.

Except Ruby Red.

SQUARK

Around the woodheap goes Banjo.
Bark. Bark. Bark.

Ruby Red ruffles her feathers.
Bark. Bark. Bark.

Ruby Red stretches her neck
and stares at the sky.
Bark. Bark. Bark.

Banjo leaps.
Logs tumble.
Sticks fly.

Ruby Red rises.
Up, up, up,

and then down into the chook shed, onto her perch.

But one day, as Banjo is rounding up the chooks,
no Ruby Red.

No chook up on the woodheap,
ruffling her feathers and staring at the sky.

Banjo slides on his belly.
He sniffs the long grass.

No Ruby Red.

He snuffles around the shed door.

No Ruby Red.

He even goes through the lambing yard and under the woolshed.

And there he finds her, lying still, her feathers flat, her eyes closed.

He takes her in his mouth and carries her to his kennel.

He places her inside and then lies down,
wrapping his body around her, close and warm.

For two days she stays there and Banjo watches over her.

On the third day she lifts her head and peers out of the kennel.

On the fourth day she stands up and pecks at some seeds.

On the fifth day she scratches at the ground and goes as far as the fence.

Today it's my job to shut up the chooks.
I whistle and yell, 'Go, Banjo, go!'

Bark. Bark. Bark.
Squark. Squark. Squark.

Chooks fly up from the grass, down from
the trees and out of the shed.

Except Ruby Red.

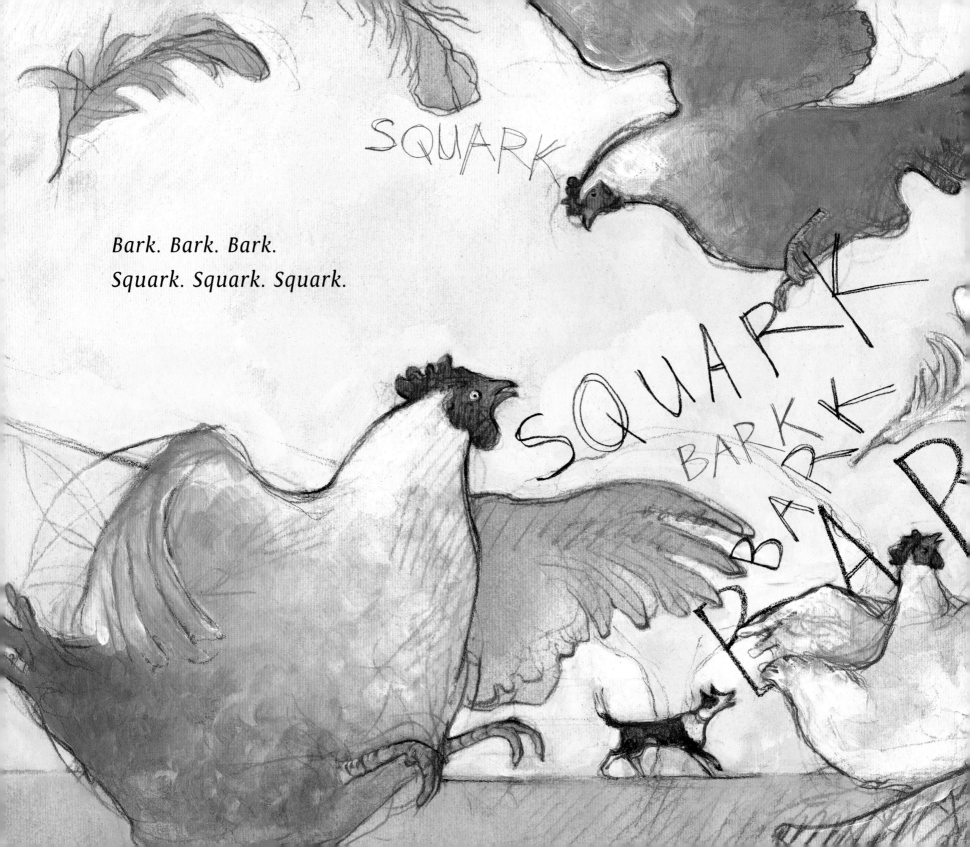

Bark. Bark. Bark.
Squark. Squark. Squark.

SQUARK

Chooks fly into the yard,
peck at the ground
and settle on their roosts.

Except Ruby Red.